Emilia Alzate-Hur

Emilia
Alzate-Hurtado

A Precious Moments Christmas
Two Classic Holiday Carols

Phillips Brooks

Martin Luther

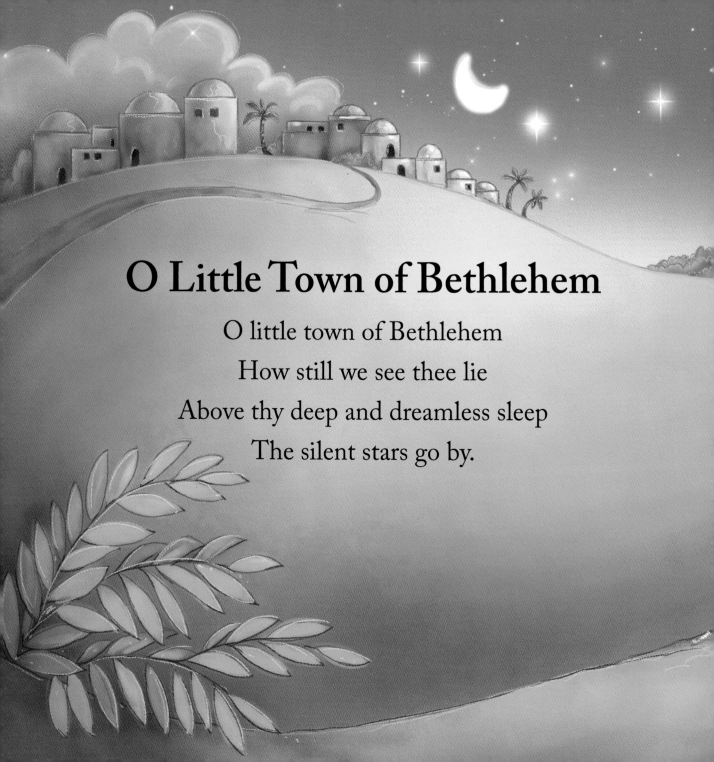

O Little Town of Bethlehem

O little town of Bethlehem

How still we see thee lie

Above thy deep and dreamless sleep

The silent stars go by.

Yet in thy dark streets shineth
The everlasting Light
The hopes and fears of all the years
Are met in thee tonight.

For Christ is born of Mary
And gathered all above
While mortals sleep, the angels keep
Their watch of wondering love.

O morning stars together
Proclaim the holy birth
And praises sing to God the King
And Peace to men on earth.

How silently, how silently
The wondrous gift is given
So God imparts to human hearts
The blessings of His heaven.

No ear may hear His coming
But in this world of sin
Where meek souls will receive him still
The dear Christ enters in.

O holy Child of Bethlehem
Descend to us, we pray
Cast out our sin and enter in
Be born to us today.

We hear the Christmas angels
The great glad tidings tell
O come to us, abide with us
Our Lord Emmanuel.

Away in a Manger

Away in a manger
No crib for His bed
The little Lord Jesus
Laid down His sweet head.

The stars in the heavens
Looked down where He lay
The little Lord Jesus
Asleep on the hay.

The cattle are lowing
The poor Baby wakes
But little Lord Jesus
No crying He makes.

I love Thee, Lord Jesus
Look down from the sky

And stay by my side
'Til morning is nigh.

Be near me, Lord Jesus,
I ask Thee to stay
Close by me forever
And love me, I pray.

Bless all the dear children
In Thy tender care
And take us to heaven
To live with Thee there.

Published by Sourcebooks Jabberwocky, an imprint of Sourcebooks, Inc.

P.O. Box 4410, Naperville, Illinois 60567-4410
(630) 961-3900
Fax: (630) 961-2168
sourcebooks.com

Source of Production: 1010 Printing Asia Limited, North Point, Hong Kong, China
Date of Production: May 2020
Run Number: 5018877

Printed and bound in China.
OGP 10 9 8 7 6 5 4 3